DENNIS

Based on *The Railway Series* by the Rev. W. Awdry

Illustrations by
Robin Davies and Jerry Smith

EGMONT

EGMONT

We bring stories to life

First published in Great Britain in 2007
by Egmont UK Limited
239 Kensington High Street, London W8 6SA
This edition published in 2008
All Rights Reserved

HiT entertainment

ISBN 978 1 4052 3495 5
1 3 5 7 9 10 8 6 4 2
Printed in Italy

The Forest Stewardship Council (FSC) is an international, non-governmental organisation dedicated to promoting responsible management of the world's forests. FSC operates a system of forest certification and product labelling that allows consumers to identify wood and wood-based products from well managed forests.

For more information about Egmont's paper buying policy please visit www.egmont.co.uk/ethicalpublishing

For more information about the FSC please visit their website at www.fsc.uk.org

*T*his is a story about Dennis, a very lazy diesel engine. On his first day on the Sodor Railway, Dennis played a trick on Thomas. But when he really got into trouble, was anyone there to help?

One morning, The Fat Controller came to Tidmouth Sheds with important news.

"A new diesel engine is coming to our Railway," he boomed. "His name is Dennis. And Thomas," added The Fat Controller, "you have been working very hard. Today, you can have a day off!"

Thomas was very pleased. "First, I will have a long washdown," chuffed Thomas, cheerfully.

On his way to the washdown, Thomas saw a diesel he had never seen before. The diesel was huffing and puffing.

"Peep! Peep!" said Thomas. "You must be Dennis! What's the matter?"

"These trucks are too troublesome. I can't shunt them," huffed Dennis.

"It's my day off," whistled Thomas. "But I'll help you."

Dennis watched Thomas biff and bump the trucks into line.

"All done," puffed Thomas.

It was hard work. When he had finished, he was very tired.

"Thank you, Thomas," said Dennis.

And he watched Thomas chuff away.

Thomas arrived at the washdown. Soon he was covered in big bubbles. Thomas was feeling very jolly on his day off.

He started puffing to himself . . .

"Shiny and bright, shiny and bright. That's what I'll be, to start my day right!" he chirruped, cheerfully.

Dennis wasn't cheerful, at all. He didn't want to deliver his trucks of tiles.

Just then, Thomas puffed into view, looking shiny and clean. Dennis had an idea. He would ask Thomas to help him again.

"Help! Help!" Dennis called, weakly. "I don't know how to get to the schoolhouse!"

"Don't worry, Dennis," said Thomas, slowing down. "I'll show you the way."

Dennis smiled – his trick had worked!

Thomas showed Dennis the way to the junction and wheeshed away.

Dennis had wanted Thomas to take his trucks for him. Suddenly, Dennis had another idea – a very naughty idea.

He blasted his horn . . . again . . . and again . . . and again . . .

Thomas heard the noise and raced back.

"Help!" cried Dennis. "I'm overheating! You will have to shunt these trucks for me!"

Thomas knew it was his day off, but he still wanted to help.

"Don't worry," puffed Thomas. "I'll find another engine to help you on my way to Bluff's Cove." And Thomas hurried away.

Dennis was cross! He uncoupled himself from the trucks. "Now another engine will have to take them!" he thought.

Dennis sped away. He didn't care about the tiles. And he didn't care about Thomas. All he cared about was getting far away from his work.

His wheels were spinning faster . . . and faster . . . and then there was trouble!

"Help!" screeched Dennis. "Help! Please, help!"

Dennis crashed right off the tracks. But this time, there was no one there to hear his cries.

When, Thomas arrived at a signal, Percy had some important news.

"The workmen are waiting for Dennis to bring the tiles to repair the school roof! The children can't go to school until it's mended!" grumbled Percy. "And no one knows where Dennis is!"

"I do!" wheeshed Thomas. "He's broken down. I must go back to help him!"

Thomas found Dennis wheel-deep in a muddy ditch.

"I thought you broke down at the junction!" huffed Thomas. "And where are the trucks?"

Dennis looked very shamefaced! He felt bad for what he had done.

"I tricked you!" said Dennis, quietly. "There was nothing wrong with me at the junction. I didn't want to pull those heavy trucks! I'm a Really Lazy Engine," sniffed Dennis.

Dennis' wheels wobbled . . . his diesel oil dripped . . . and he had a very long face!

Thomas decided to help one more time.

"I'll pull you back on to the tracks," puffed Thomas. "Then I'll be your back engine. That way we'll get the tiles to the schoolhouse really quickly!"

Dennis smiled his biggest smile ever. "Thank you, Thomas," he said.

A little later, Dennis and Thomas pulled into the schoolhouse station. The Fat Controller was very cross with Dennis.

"I'm sorry," said Dennis. He felt terrible. "Thomas has shown me that being a Really Useful Engine is much better than being a Really Lazy one," wheeshed Dennis.

The Fat Controller was pleased when Dennis said sorry. And Thomas wasn't cross any more.

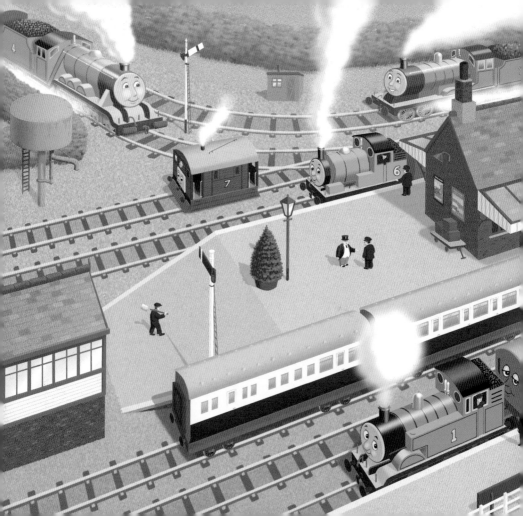

The Thomas Story Library is THE definitive collection of stories about Thomas and ALL his friends.

5 more Thomas Story Library titles will be chuffing into your local bookshop in August 2008!

Jeremy
Hector
BoCo
Billy
Whiff

And there are even more Thomas Story Library books to follow late

So go on, start your Thomas Story Library NOW!

A Fantastic Offer for Thomas the Tank Engine Fans!

In every Thomas Story Library book like this one, you will find a special token. Collect 6 Thomas tokens and we will send you a brilliant Thomas poster, and a double-sided bedroom door hanger! Simply tape a £1 coin in the space above, and fill out the form overleaf.

TO BE COMPLETED BY AN ADULT

To apply for this great offer, ask an adult to complete the coupon below and send it with a pound coin and 6 tokens, to:
THOMAS OFFERS, PO BOX 715, HORSHAM RH12 5WG

☐ Please send a Thomas poster and door hanger. I enclose 6 tokens plus a £1 coin. (Price includes P&P)

Fan's name...

Address...

....Postcode...........................

Date of birth..

Name of parent/guardian...

Signature of parent/guardian...

Please allow 28 days for delivery. Offer is only available while stocks last. We reserve the right to change the terms of this offer at any time and we offer a 14 day money back guarantee. This does not affect your statutory rights.

☐ Data Protection Act: If you do not wish to receive other similar offers from us or companies we recommend, please tick this box. Offers apply to UK only.